Seaside
SANCTUARY

Seaside Sanctuary is published by Stone Arch Books
A Capstone Imprint
1710 Roe Crest Drive
North Mankato, Minnesota 56003
www.mycapstone.com

Library of Congress Cataloging-in-Publication Data
Names: Berne, Emma Carlson, author. | Madrid, Erwin, illustrator.
Title: Orca in open water / by Emma Carlson Berne ; illustrated by Erwin Madrid.
Description: North Mankato, Minnesota : Stone Arch Books, [2019] | Series: Seaside sanctuary | Summary: Elsa Roth and her best friend, Olivia, are accompanying Elsa's mother on an expedition to study the diet of orcas in the San Juan Island in the Pacific Northwest, where they are soon caught up in the drama surrounding August, a young orca calf, who has gotten separated from his pod—the marine mammal sanctuary wants to rescue and rehabilitate him for a quick return to his own pod when they can be found, but the local Oceanarium wants to keep him for display.
Identifiers: LCCN 2018044108 | ISBN 9781496578624 (hardcover) | ISBN 9781496580313 (pbk.) | ISBN 9781496578662 (ebook pdf)
Subjects: LCSH: Killer whale—Juvenile fiction. | Marine parks and reserves—Juvenile fiction. | Wildlife rescue—Juvenile fiction. | Public aquariums—Juvenile fiction. | Captive marine mammals—Juvenile fiction. | Aquatic animal welfare—Juvenile fiction. | San Juan Island (Wash.)—Juvenile fiction. | CYAC: Killer whale—Fiction. | Whales—Fiction. | Marine parks and reserves—Fiction. | Wildlife rescue—Fiction. | Amusement parks—Fiction. | Animals—Treatment—Fiction. | San Juan Island (Wash.)—Fiction.
Classification: LCC PZ7.B455139 Or 2019 | DDC 813.6 [Fic]—dc23
LC record available at https://lccn.loc.gov/2018044108

Designer: Aruna Rangarajan
Photo Credits: Shutterstock: AnSuArt, 109, Color Brush, design element throughout, KRAUCHANKA HENADZ, design element throughout, Nikiparonak, design element throughout, Theeradech Sanin, design element throughout

Special thanks to Wayne McFee, research wildlife biologist at the National Oceanic and Atmospheric Administration's National Ocean Service, for his advice and guidance on the world of dolphins and their rehabilitation. The author is very grateful.

The events in this book were inspired by the true story of Springer, an orphaned orca rescued off Puget Sound and eventually released near Vancouver Island. Springer was reunited with her pod and thrived. She is the only orca known to have been captured by humans and successfully returned to the wild.

Printed in the United States of America. PA49

Orca in
Open Water

by Emma Carlson Berne
illustrated by Erwin Madrid

STONE ARCH BOOKS
a capstone imprint

Dear Diary,

The past few months have been crazy, and not just because I moved across the country. I never thought we'd leave Chicago. The city was home my whole life. I loved the rumbling above-ground trains, the massive skyscrapers, the sidewalks filled with people. . . . Believe it or not, I even liked my school. It was the type of place where it was cool to be smart.

But then, right after school ended for the year, Mom and Dad announced we were moving. They decided to leave their jobs as marine biologists at the Shedd Aquarium and move the whole family to Charleston, South Carolina! They both got jobs running someplace called Seaside Sanctuary Marine Wildlife Refuge—jobs that were "too good to pass up," as they put it.

And at first, I couldn't believe Seaside Sanctuary would ever seem like home. Everything was different—the humidity, the salty air, the palmetto trees, the old brick streets lined with massive live oaks. Not to mention the flat, quiet beaches with water warm enough to swim in all year—you don't see that along Lake Michigan.

But it hasn't all been bad. For starters, I met my best friend, Olivia, on my first day at Seaside Sanctuary. She was sitting by the turtle pool, reading. By the end of the morning, I knew three very important things about Olivia:

1. Her older sister, Abby, is the vet at the sanctuary.
2. She doesn't like talking to people she doesn't know.
3. She wants to be a dolphin researcher when she grows up.

And I knew we were going to be best friends.

I still miss Chicago. But between helping the volunteers with feedings, cleaning tanks, showing tourists around, and prepping seal food in the industrial-sized blender, I haven't had much time to think about my old life. And one thing is for sure—at Seaside Sanctuary, I'm never lonely, and I'm never bored.

Chapter 1

"Let's move out!" the captain shouted. The sharp blast of a horn sounded over the Puget Sound Harbor. The engines rumbled beneath my feet, and the *Marie Curie*, the research boat I was standing on, pulled away from the dock.

I glanced over at Olivia, and we tightened our fingers on the metal railings of the bow of the ship. I couldn't believe where we were. We'd flown out to the state of Washington—clear across the country from Charleston—two days ago. We weren't alone, of course. My mom was there too. She was taking part in a month-long expedition to study the diet of orca whales near the San Juan Islands.

When Mom first told me where she was going, I thought she'd meant somewhere in the Caribbean. But it turned out that the San Juan Islands were in the Pacific Northwest, off the coast of Washington. And when I found out the expedition was during summer break, I begged her to let Olivia and me come along. After what seemed like weeks of talking and phone calls and forms, the three of us boarded a plane for Seattle.

The minute my sneakers crunched on the gravel path of the San Juan Marine Mammal Sanctuary, I felt like I was back at home. The outdoor pools for the small seals, the otter habitat, the big pool for rehabbing dolphins—if I closed my eyes, I might as well have been back at Seaside Sanctuary. They even had a wild sea pen, just like we did back home, with netting strung across a natural cove. We were one of only a few sanctuaries in the country to have one—apparently SJS was another.

There were a few differences that made it clear I was no longer on the Carolina coast. For one thing, SJS only took mammals, so they didn't have bird pens or turtle tanks like we did. And the air smelled different—colder, even like snow sometimes. There were rocks everywhere, where we had sand and grasses, and the ocean was rough and cold-looking and deep. Pine trees clung to the rocks and leaned over the sea. The ocean was far down the cliffs, above which were all the roads and houses. You couldn't just stroll down to the water the way you could in Charleston.

Finally the expedition was underway. I was so excited that I'd barely slept the night before. But we were really on the ship now, bright red life jackets strapped on, engines vibrating beneath our feet, cold spray hitting our faces, the dark, sloshing ocean unrolling in front of us.

"When can we start looking for orcas?" I called to Mom. She was standing beside Arden Harrington, the head marine biologist at SJS. They were both looking through giant black binoculars mounted to the railing of the deck. They were the biggest binoculars I'd ever seen. They had to be two feet long.

"As soon as you can!" Arden called back. She smiled at us. "Every pair of eyes helps. We're trying to find pod J34. We were able to attach a satellite tag to one of the orcas in that pod last year. The tag sends signals to a satellite, which sends a message to a transmitter on the ground. Then the transmitting station sends us an email with the pod's location. We've gotten the GPS coordinates. That should tell us where to look for the pod."

"Pods are orca family groups, right?" Olivia said.

We'd both done some orca-related reading on the plane ride out here. To my surprise, I'd learned that orcas aren't actually whales at all. They're the largest members of the dolphin family.

"Right," Mom said, coming over to us. "Orcas live and hunt in really tight family groups, just like humans. They stay together for their entire lives. In fact, male orcas never leave their mothers. They go away to mate, but they always come back."

"Wow!" I said. "That is so cool."

"It really is," Arden chimed in. "They're the only mammals known to do that in the world, including humans."

"You're not going to catch me living with *my* mom my whole life," said a voice from behind us.

I turned around and saw a skinny guy about my age coming out of the cabin. He was wearing three sets of regular-sized binoculars around his neck and had a mop of dark hair. His skin was deeply tanned, as if he'd spent many hours outside.

"Oh please. You know you can't get enough of me," Arden said. She swatted playfully at his head. "Elsa and Olivia, meet Cooper. He's my son and resident troublemaker."

"Thanks a lot, Mom. What an introduction." Cooper rolled his eyes, and everyone laughed.

Cooper made his way over to where Olivia and I were standing by the railing. "I'm Cooper," he said. "Ach, my mom just said that." He hit himself comically in the forehead with the heel of his hand.

"Nice to meet you," I replied. "I'm Elsa, and this is Olivia."

"Want some binoculars?" Cooper offered. He took off two of the pairs of binoculars and handed them to us.

"Thanks," I said. "We'll be able to see a lot better now." I slipped the binoculars over my neck before asking, "Do you live at SJS?"

Cooper shook his head. "I wish. My mom and I live off-site. But I come over all the time." He leaned his forearms on the metal railing and focused the binoculars on the ocean. "So did Mom bring you up to date on what we're looking for?"

"Yeah." I brought my own binoculars up to my eyes. "She said we're looking for J34 pod. They tagged one of the orcas in that group last year, right?"

"Yep." Cooper nodded. "They want to see what they're eating, mainly," he told us, still peering through his binoculars. "And they want to take weather and temperature readings to study the environment where the orcas are spending their time."

Olivia and I looked at each other. "You must like orcas," I said. "You know a lot about them."

"Yeah." Cooper's face turned slightly red, and he cleared his throat. "I want to be a marine biologist one day. Anyway, orcas are so cool. Wait until you see your first pod."

I appreciated Cooper's enthusiasm. He seemed nice. Like someone I'd be friends with back at home even.

Just then Mom came up behind us, pausing on her way back to the cabin. "Keep your eyes peeled for a small orca in particular. Arden says that should be J-50," she said. "He's the youngest member of the pod. At least he was last year. He's the son of J-16. We want to see how he's kept up with the group this year. He was tagged as well, so we'll be able to identify him fairly easily."

I pressed my binoculars against my eye sockets and stared eagerly at the gray water. I knew I probably wouldn't be able to see the tag from the boat, but maybe I could still spot a dorsal fin. I stood there for what felt like forever but nothing, nothing, nothing.

My face was wet from spray, and my hands were growing cramped. I was chilly too, even though it was summer, but I didn't want to take a break to go into the cabin. I might miss something.

"A fin!" Olivia shrieked beside me.

Quickly I focused my binoculars in the direction she was looking. Sure enough, a gray fin was poking up above the water.

"False alarm," I said, lowering my binoculars. "It's a bottlenose dolphin."

Cooper looked too. "It looks kind of like a shark to me," he said.

"Ah, no," I said. Cooper looked over at me. "It's definitely a dolphin."

"How do you know?" His tone was faintly challenging.

"Well, for one thing, the fin is curved. If it was a shark, it would be an exact triangle shape. And for another, you can see the fin swooping up and down. That's the dolphin swimming. A shark fin would cut straight across the top of the water, because sharks swim differently," I finished.

Cooper was staring at me with his mouth slightly open. He shut it abruptly. "Oh," was all he said.

Suddenly Mom rushed out from the cabin where she'd been looking at the GPS with the captain. "We just got the updated coordinates," she said, grabbing her own binoculars and peering through them. "The captain's going to start heading that direction right now."

I quickly turned and stared back at the ocean as if I could will the whale to appear. I wanted to be the first one to spot him. Olivia crowded beside me, looking too.

"He'll be with the rest of the pod and his mother," Mom said. "The other tag in the pod isn't picking up. But it could just be a technical glitch. Tags can sometimes fall off or stop transmitting."

For a few more minutes, we rumbled through the water. Everyone was silent and focused.

"There!" Cooper exclaimed, pointing. "I see one!"

I focused as well, and a thrill went through me when I saw the curved black back and tall dorsal fin. A plume of water spray surrounded it. Some Native American tribes called orcas "blackfish," and I could see why.

"And the rest of the pod . . ." Mom's voice trailed off. She was silent for a minute, searching the water.

I searched too. But then Mom lowered her binoculars. I was already thinking what she said next: "He's alone. The rest of the pod's nowhere to be seen."

Chapter 2

"Where are they? Where is his mother?" Olivia asked.

We were all clustered at the railing now: Arden, Cooper, Mom, Olivia, and me. At Mom's request, the captain had idled the boat, and we could clearly see the little orca, diving around us—alone.

Mom shook her head slowly. "I don't know. But this isn't good. Orca mothers never leave their calves, and they would certainly never leave the pod voluntarily."

Arden spoke up, looking concerned. "We've seen this before, unfortunately. The only time we see an orca calf alone is when the mother has died."

"But what about the rest of the pod?" I asked her.

"Pods never leave calves behind on purpose," Arden replied. "Since the J34 pod is nowhere to be seen, I can only assume he lost them after his mother died. In the past, when orca calves were captured, the adults would surround the nets and call and call for the babies who were being taken away on boats. The only way this calf would be on his own is by accident."

"So he's all alone?" I asked, looking at the little fin swimming around us. The ocean suddenly seemed very big and very lonely.

"It looks that way," Mom said, studying the orca carefully. "Do you see how he's swimming so close to the boat? Orphaned orcas get lonely. They'll swim right up and bump against boats as a kind of substitute for other orcas. It's dangerous to have them get so close. They can get hurt. And people can try to touch or capture them."

"What are we going to do?" Cooper asked. I could hear the urgency in his voice.

"I'm honestly not sure," Arden said. "Orphans don't show up that often. It's a sad fact, but they usually die before humans spot them."

"What about the J34 pod?" I said. "If we can find his family, we could reunite them."

Mom was focusing her binoculars on the calf again. "We'll need to pause our search for the time being. We need to concentrate on what do about this little guy first."

We watched the little orca breaching in the water—jumping up and splashing back down. He blew a fine spray of water out of the blowhole at the top of his head.

I knew already that the blowhole was his nose. It was on top instead of in the front of his face, so he could breathe without poking his head out of the water.

"You see how the area behind his blowhole is sunken?" Arden said, looking closely. "That's called peanut-head."

"What does it mean?" Cooper asked. "Is that bad?"

Arden looked serious. "It means he's very, very hungry. Starving, in fact. Orcas store fat behind their blowholes. When the area is sunken like that, it means he's using up his fat stores." She focused the binoculars again. We all did the same. "And do you see how his back looks sunken on either side of his spine? That's another sign he's very, very thin. Too thin."

"Will he be OK?" I asked, leaning over the railing until the metal dug into my stomach. "Hey! Hey, little guy!" I called to him. Turning back to the people on the boat I said, "We should give him a name."

"August?" Olivia said. "For the month we found him?"

"I like that," I said.

Mom was only half-listening to the naming discussion we were having. She and Arden exchanged a look. Finally Arden spoke gently, replying to my original question.

"I'm going to be honest with you kids. If he doesn't get help he likely won't be OK," she said. "Mother orcas teach their babies to hunt. They teach them the culture of the pod. They have their own dialect of the orca language. Orcas are highly social. Without a pod and a mother to teach him, he'll almost certainly die of starvation and isolation."

"No!" Cooper burst out. "We can't let that happen to August."

"And we're not going to," Mom reassured us. "But we need to get back to shore and make some calls." She signaled through the window of the bridge, and the captain turned the boat around.

"Wait!" Olivia said. "How will we find him again?"

"We'll use the tracker," Mom said. "Just like before."

All the way back to shore, I couldn't think of anything but that little calf, alone and lost, wondering where his mother is.

"We have to save him!" I murmured to Olivia. "We just have to!"

She looked at me with the same distress I was feeling inside. On the other side, Cooper scowled. "We will. I know we will."

If only I could feel so sure.

Chapter 3

I felt more hopeful when we got back to SJS. We all piled into the shed they used for an office, and Mom and Arden got on the phones. In no time at all, the office had filled up with officials.

There were two scientists from NOAA— the National Oceanic and Atmospheric Administration. I knew that they were kind of like the government representatives for the ocean. Someone from the Washington governor's office showed up too. There was also a man from San Juan Islands Oceanarium. Cooper explained briefly that it was a big local marine park. I'd heard of it before, but we didn't have one anywhere near Charleston.

Arden filled them in on everything we'd seen out on the boat. Then everyone started talking, passing papers back and forth.

Finally the governor's rep, a tall man with short, curly hair, spoke up. "So what are you proposing?" he asked.

Mom shot Arden a look. "We'd like support for a rescue, followed by a short-term rehabilitation and the return of August to his pod," she said. "We'll hopefully have located them by the time he's ready to be released."

There was a rustle in the room. I didn't see anything crazy about what Mom had said, but the other adults were glancing at each other uneasily.

"You know as well as we do that an orca has never been successfully released back into the wild," the Oceanarium rep said. "Five years ago, Oceanarium released an orca that had been a part of our shows. He was too comfortable with humans. He kept coming back to us for food and companionship. A year later, he died of pneumonia."

An angry look crossed Mom's face. "I know the orca you're talking about, Davis. We all do." She looked deeply upset as she spoke. "That whale was raised in captivity by Oceanarium after being kidnapped from his pod as a calf. He spent his entire life at your theme park, living in unnatural conditions in tanks and pools and being forced to perform. You only released him after intense public pressure. Of course he didn't survive! He'd never lived in the wild. He was never given the chance!"

The air in the room felt charged, as if filled with electricity. Davis and the government official glanced at each other uneasily. But the others were nodding, their lips pressed together.

"Whoa," Cooper muttered on one side of me. "Your mom *really* doesn't like Oceanarium."

"I know," I whispered back. "But can you blame her?"

"I'd like to request the orphan be rehabbed at Oceanarium," Davis said, ignoring Mom's fury. "He can't possibly be returned to his pod after contact with humans. It's never been done! What you're suggesting could kill him. Our facilities are state-of-the-art. We'll take good care of him."

Mom shook her head, but before she could speak again, Arden jumped in. "SJS has one of the only wild pens in the country," she said. "It's big enough to house August for a short time. NOAA can oversee the rehab. He'll be released as soon as he's well and we find his pod. We're still working out the details, but we want a chance to try."

"What about the danger to his life?" Davis challenged.

Mom didn't say anything. She looked at Arden.

"You're right that this is risky," Arden said quietly. "And it's true that an orca has never been successfully released into the wild after rehab by humans. August could die from stress or injury during the process. But if we do nothing, he'll die slowly from disease and starvation. And at Oceanarium, he'll be condemned to a life as a trained animal. That's inhumane."

Davis opened his mouth to speak, clearly ready to defend Oceanarium. But before he could, the government official held up his hand.

"Thank you, all," he said. "I understand this is a difficult issue. We clearly all feel strongly about it. For the time being, the state will support NOAA in a rescue. The orca will be taken to SJS for rehab and release. Let's make the necessary preparations."

Mom, Arden, Cooper, Olivia, and I all broke into huge smiles. Olivia squeezed my hand. Success!

Not everyone was as happy, though. Davis swept his papers into a pile and left the room without saying goodbye to anyone. But in the doorway, he paused and gave Mom a long stare. I had an uneasy feeling that we hadn't seen the last of him—or Oceanarium.

Out in the strong Washington wind, Cooper, Olivia, and I crunched down the gravel path after Arden. Mom and the NOAA reps stayed behind to make calls.

We scrambled down a long, winding path leading from the cliff on which SJS was perched to the small cove with the wild pen. The SJS boats were pulled up on the sand.

Arden started untangling a length of rope. "We'll take two of these small boats to the rescue, so let's clear some of this stuff out."

"Arden, is Oceanarium really that bad?" I asked her as we clustered around one of the small boats. "That guy said their place is state-of-the-art. Would it be so awful if August had to go there?"

"Oceanarium is a company whose goal is to make money," Arden said. She looked as upset as Mom had sounded. "They capture young mammals, like bottlenose dolphins and orcas, plus other animals like seals, and train them to do tricks in shows. It's not natural for the animals, and it's cruel. But Oceanarium argues that these animals are safer in captivity. And they do have vets on staff and money to spend."

Arden paused and looked at us, like she wanted us to understand how important her words were. "But a tank is still a tank, no matter how nice it is."

Chapter 4

"Elsa! Olivia!" Cooper's voice cut through the darkness of the guesthouse. For a moment I burrowed further into my blankets. Then suddenly, I sat up and clawed the covers from my head.

Today was the day. It was time to rescue August.

For three days, we'd been going out in small boats and idling next to the little orca. We'd been trying to get him used to us and the boats by floating a small chunk of log attached to a cord over the side. The log was like a signal of our presence, Arden had said. August would squeak when he saw the log and come up to the boat. Then we'd reach over the sides to touch his fins, and, when he'd turn over, rub his belly.

At first I'd been confused. I thought the whole point was that we *didn't* want August to get used to boats or humans. But Mom had explained that we had to do it to prepare him for the actual rescue. If he was used to us and our boats, he'd be quieter and more willing during the rescue. Then he'd be less likely to hurt himself or one of us.

Olivia rolled out of the top bunk, and in the darkness, we pulled on jeans and heavy sweatshirts against the pre-dawn chill. Then we hurried out to meet Cooper.

"Is everything ready?" I asked him as we crunched down the steep path to the beach.

"Yeah, your mom and my mom have been down there for an hour. The NOAA scientists too," he said. "We've got to get this rescue done today. We can't delay anymore. The longer we wait, the weaker August is getting. He won't last much longer."

"Let's move out!" Arden called as we came up to the boats. "Olivia and Elsa in with me. Cooper, you can go with Dr. Roth." The two NOAA scientists, Jason and Greg, each climbed aboard one of the boats. Jason was wearing a wet suit and carrying a pair of flippers.

"All right, listen up!" Greg instructed us as the boats motored slowly out of the cove. "Our colleagues will meet us on a crane boat out where we expect to find August. We'll use a tail rope to gently position him between the two boats. We'll need to hold him steady while the orca stretcher is maneuvered beneath him and attached to the crane. Then the crane will lift him onto the crane boat."

"Then what?" I asked.

"Then he'll ride on the crane boat back to SJS. The crane boat will be staffed with NOAA trained volunteers and biologists. They'll monitor his vital signs the whole way."

We all nodded. I searched for Olivia's hand in the darkness and gripped it. Her eyes were gleaming. I wasn't sure if this was the greatest adventure of our lives, but it was sure close.

Arden leaned forward. Her face was serious. "I want you girls to be ready. This rescue is extremely risky. August could hurt himself thrashing. We could accidentally hurt him as we move him. The stress alone could kill him."

Olivia nodded. "We're ready," she whispered.

The boats picked up speed as we moved across the open ocean. The cold, wet air blew against my face as the boats cut through the water. The day was calm. In the eastern sky, a pink glow grew steadily brighter.

After half an hour, Mom waved her arm at us from the other boat. "We've located August's tag," she called. "He's in the same spot as before. He's probably not strong enough to swim far at this point. I've radioed the crane boat to meet us."

I exhaled. We'd found him. One hurdle passed.

Twenty minutes later, I saw the big red-and-white crane boat, its giant arm sticking up from the deck. It looked intimidating, but I reminded myself that it was the only chance August had at survival.

Arden and Mom slowed the boats, then cut the engines to idle so that we were only rocking on the waves. We waved to the crew on the crane boat, and they waved back.

Mom threw out the log on the rope. Two seconds later, I spotted August's back and dorsal fin, swimming in a slow circle.

"He's tired," Arden said. "See how slowly he's going? And he's not diving or breaching. He's exhausted and starving. He doesn't have energy to do anything more than stay at the surface."

"We're here, boy!" I called to August. "Please, let us help you."

"Throw the log," Arden instructed.

I picked up the wet section of log from where it sat on the floor and tossed it in. One end was tethered to the side of the boat. August immediately swam over to it.

"OK, let's get this started," Greg called. "This is it, folks."

My heartbeat picked up. I clutched Olivia's arm. She shot me a nervous look in return.

Mom maneuvered her boat closer to August, and Jason carefully got to his feet. He threw out a soft, stretchy piece of white rope and landed a loop neatly around August's tail. He pulled, and the knot tightened.

Almost immediately August squealed and tried to swim away.

"Oh!" I exclaimed.

"It's OK," Olivia said. "It's not hurting him. He just doesn't like being held."

"I know . . ." She was right, but it was still hard. My eyes were glued to the scene in front of us.

Very gently, Jason towed August so that he was up against the side of their boat. August was chirping and calling and thrashing.

"Quick!" Jason called to Arden. "Steer over!"

Arden moved our boat into position, so that August was between the long sides of both boats. Greg leaned over and unrolled the orca stretcher from the side of our boat. It was a long black sling of tough cloth with two metal poles on either side. There were holes, lined with padding, cut out for August's fins.

"OK, Jason, we're ready for you!" Greg called.

Jason zipped his wet suit up to his neck and put on his flippers. Then he eased over the edge of the boat and into the water. He swam around the side of the boat and secured the stretcher to the other boat.

"This is going great, girls," Greg reassured us, leaning over the boat. "I know August seems stressed, but he's actually being quite calm. He's not very strong, which helps."

Cooper, Olivia, and I didn't want to call out, but we sent silent, *I hope this works* messages with our eyes. It was all we could do.

The adults were all focused on their jobs. Every ounce of Mom and Arden's energy was on keeping the boats in exactly the right position. Greg maneuvered August toward the stretcher, while in the water, Jason steadied and guided the orca. August squeaked wildly, but the adults were calm as the little whale slid forward onto the partially submerged sling of cloth.

Everyone breathed a sigh of relief. August was in the stretcher. We'd passed another hurdle.

Chapter 5

The crane boat moved slowly toward us, and as we watched, the crew dropped two heavy cables over the side. Both were made of twisted metal and had big metal hooks on either end. The cables were attached to the massive crane itself.

Jason climbed back in the boat. He and Greg quickly fastened the hooks to loops on either end of the stretcher.

"Bring it up!" he shouted to the crane boat crew. They waved and slowly began winching the stretcher into the air.

"Come on, August!" I muttered. "Please stay still."

The stretcher came out of the water like a dripping black bundle. August was suspended in the air. He couldn't move much because of the pressure of the stretcher around his body. Slowly the crane lifted him into the air. Then, with a grinding of gears, it turned him toward the crane boat itself.

"Think of how surprised he must be," Olivia said. "He probably never thought he'd be hanging out mid-air."

Slowly the stretcher was lowered onto the deck of the crane boat. He'd only been in the air for about thirty seconds.

"Come on!" Jason was motioning to Olivia and me. "You guys want to ride with August? I'm going to ride with him, and we could use the extra hands."

We looked at Arden. "Go ahead!" Arden said. "August knows you. You can comfort him on the ride back."

Arden held the small boat steady as Olivia and I scrambled carefully out of the boat after Jason and climbed up iron ladders on the side of the crane boat. I could see Cooper in the other boat doing the same thing.

When we were all on board we turned and waved goodbye. Mom and Arden waved back, then disappeared over the waves as we turned all our attention to August.

The little orca had been lowered onto a foam pad that was about three feet thick. Jason and the rest of the crew were working quickly to unfasten the stretcher. They took off the metal poles and let the whole contraption hang down.

Quickly the crew swooped in to examine him. The vet took blood samples near his fin and listened to his side with a stethoscope. I saw him swab the inside of August's blowhole and eyes and put the swabs in a vial. Then he felt August all over with his hands, squeezing and prodding him.

"Is he going to be OK out of the water?" I asked anxiously. August looked so different lying there, out in the air.

"He will as long as we keep him wet, cool, and calm," Jason assured me. "That's where you guys come in."

"OK." Olivia nodded. "What do you need us to do?"

Jason handed an armful of thin white cloths to Cooper and a big bucket of water to Olivia. "This is seawater," he told them. "Cooper, you're going to lay the cloths over August's back and head and flippers. Not his face. They'll keep him from getting sunburned on the boat ride back. Olivia, you pour water over him as much as you can. That will cool him and keep his skin from drying out."

"What about me?" I asked.

Jason positioned me by August's head. "Elsa, you're in charge of keeping him calm. Get your head down there where he can see you and talk to him. Pat him, tell him he's going to be OK. He'll recognize your voice."

The big boat revved up its engine, and I felt us start moving forward in the water. Instinctively, I put my hand on August's head as Cooper and Olivia got busy with the cloths.

"Hey, buddy," I said softly, crouching down. I pulled up a nearby crate and perched on it so my face was right next to August's. "How are you doing?"

The little orca whistled, his eye turning toward me.

"I know you can hear me," I told him. "You just have to trust us. We're going to help you, not hurt you."

"How's he doing?" Cooper asked, arranging the last of the cloths on August's smooth back.

I rubbed a hand over August's skin. Touching him felt like rubbing a very firm balloon. Even out of the water, you could feel the power of his muscles beneath his skin. At that moment, Olivia poured water on the cloths from August's head to his tail. He half-closed his eyes, and I could almost hear him sigh with relief.

"He says that water feels good, and he'd like some more, please," I called back.

Olivia smiled. "Coming right up." She bustled over to a barrel of seawater in a corner of the deck.

We spent the next twenty minutes talking to August and keeping him calm and comfortable.

I felt like I couldn't look away. It was almost like I was keeping him calm and alive by watching him. Jason came by every five minutes or so with the vet and checked his vital signs.

I breathed a sigh of relief when I saw the buildings of SJS perched on their high cliff. We'd made it. August had made it.

I felt like we kept moving forward up a long staircase. At the very top was August's successful release back to his pod. But the steps to get there were so risky. On each one, we risked falling and tumbling head over heels to the bottom.

❧

The next morning, I found Cooper and Olivia near the sea pen, hanging on their stomachs over the rock edge, gazing down into the water. I'd slept like a rock after August had been unloaded yesterday. It had been a lot like the rescue, except in reverse. Jason and the others had reattached the stretcher to the crane cables. Then the crane had lifted August straight up and lowered him down into the sea pen. After they'd unhooked the stretcher, the crane boat had driven away.

August had swum around quietly, not diving or breaching. We'd watched him for a while, then Mom made me go back to the guesthouse and take a shower. She said I smelled like fish, which I didn't think was so bad.

The sea pen at SJS was a lot like the one back at Seaside Sanctuary. Nature had made a natural cove with rocks on three sides. A big net stretched across the fourth side, keeping the animal inside contained but giving it plenty of room to swim.

Wild sea pens were much better for big mammals like orcas. Mom and Dad had explained that a billion times back at Seaside Sanctuary. The animals could eat the fish that naturally swam in, they could get a lot more exercise, and the water was the right temperature and saltiness. We could feed August lots of fish here, and he'd gain weight.

"How is he doing?" I asked. I plopped down next to Olivia and wiggled over until I could peer over the edge too.

"See for yourself," Olivia said. She pointed.

August was swimming slowly around the sea pen. He wasn't diving or breaching, but he wasn't holding still either, just like yesterday.

"At least he's alive," I said, trying to sound hopeful.

"Kids!" Arden came up behind us. "Good, I'm glad you're here. I want you to see how to feed August, so you can help us later."

We scrambled up and followed Arden down the path to a wide rocky ledge about halfway down the cliff. There, a long white pipe led down into the sea pen below. A white curtain had been draped over the end of the pipe that led into the water.

Arden picked up a bucket of live salmon and handed it to Cooper. "We got the vet's report from yesterday." She smiled at us all. "You'll be glad to know that August is mainly suffering from undernourishment."

"Wait, why will we be glad to know that?" Cooper asked. "He's starving! That sounds awful."

I had been thinking just the same thing.

Arden squeezed her son's shoulder. "Because that's something we can cure. We're going to feed August lots of good fish to build up his strength."

"So if we're going to feed him, why are we all the way up here?" I asked.

"We have to send the fish down this pipe, because we don't want him to start associating the fish with humans," Arden explained. "Remember, we want him to stay wild and stay away from boats most of all. Go ahead, Cooper."

Cooper stepped forward and shot the big salmon down the pipe. Olivia and I craned our necks and saw a tiny splash far below. August swam over and dived for the fish.

"He's got it!" Olivia said. "He ate it!"

Arden grinned. "That's a good sign, because these are live fish. August needs to hunt, not just snack on dead fish that don't move. If he was staying forever here, dead fish are fine. But he's not. He's leaving."

I grinned. Arden was right. If we had anything to say about it, August would soon be back in the wild—where he belonged.

Chapter 6

Over the next week, Cooper, Olivia, and I
slid so many salmon down August's chute that my
fingers felt permanently coated with fish slime.
Not that I minded. August was getting better every
day. He was diving and breaching more frequently,
which Mom said was a sign he was getting his
energy back.

We still couldn't get too close to him, though.
Arden said he needed as little contact with people

as possible, but she looked at him every day through her high-powered binoculars.

"He's gaining weight," she said on Tuesday morning, peering down at him from our ledge. "You can see from the bigger splashes he's making. His head is losing that peanut shape."

She handed me the binoculars, and I put the strap around my neck. We were standing fifty feet up after all, and I didn't think Arden would appreciate her fancy binoculars taking a bath in the Pacific.

Once they were secure, I focused the lens and spotted August swimming around the netted section of the pen, nosing at the webbing.

"He's exploring!" I said happily. I handed the binoculars to Olivia so she could see too.

"That's a good sign, right, Mom?" Cooper asked.

"Definitely," Arden agreed. "He's a lot more active now. He has energy to explore, whereas before he didn't. I think we'll be looking at a release in another week or so, as soon as we get the OK from the vet. He needs to gain just a little more weight. He should be about six hundred pounds, so he has about twenty pounds to go."

I grinned. If August was going to be released that soon, maybe we'd get to see it before we had to head back to Charleston. It would be a dream come true to see him reunited with his pod.

After a few more minutes we headed back up the path. Halfway up, we almost collided with Mom, who was hurrying from the office with a piece of paper in her hand.

"Kids! Is Arden with you—oh, there you are!" She saw Arden behind us. "I just opened this letter. It looks serious."

Arden scanned the letter. Then she exhaled. "We'll fight it. They won't get him." She folded the paper, but I could tell she really wanted to tear it into bits. My joy at watching August eat evaporated, replaced by worry.

"Get what?" Olivia asked. At the same time, Cooper said, "Get who?"

Arden handed him the letter. "Here. You kids might as well know what we're up against."

Cooper unfolded the paper, and Olivia and I both leaned over his shoulder to read.

To: Dr. Arden Harrington

San Juan Marine Mammal Sanctuary

484 Pacific Highway No. 25

Dear Dr. Harrington:

This letter is in regard to the care and housing of orca J50 from pod J34, also known as "August." It has come to our attention that the San Juan Marine Mammal Sanctuary intends to release the young orca back into the wild. It is Oceanarium's belief that the orca will receive better care and a safer life in our premier, world-class facility. The animal will have the opportunity to receive top-grade veterinary monitoring, nutrition, and exercise in a natural setting.

To this end, we have contacted NOAA to request the release of J-50 to our care, effective immediately. NOAA has asked for a meeting, at which time the organization will make its decision. Details, we assume, will be forthcoming.

Yours sincerely,
Davis Hammond
Oceanarium Chief Orca Trainer

I couldn't believe what I was reading. Silently Mom handed Arden a second opened envelope. We read over her shoulder:

To: Dr. Arden Harrington
San Juan Marine Mammal Sanctuary
484 Pacific Highway No. 25

Dear Dr. Harrington:

Your presence is required at the offices of NOAA on Wednesday, July 14, to discuss the care and potential release of orca J-50. Officials representing the marine facility

Oceanarium will also be present to state their case.

Thank you for your cooperation in this matter.

Sincerely,

Chip Sheffield

NOAA Pacific Northwest Executive Officer

Cooper looked up. His eyes were wide. "Oceanarium is trying to take August? How can they do that? I thought this was all decided already."

I was surprised to hear a tremble in Cooper's voice. I'd thought so too.

Arden nodded. She put her arm around his shoulder. "I'm afraid so. We'll have to make the best argument we can that he belongs in the wild."

"Maybe Oceanarium *wouldn't* be so bad," Olivia said quietly. She pointed at the part about a natural setting and all the top-grade food and care. "It seems like they'd take good care of him."

"No!" Cooper's shout startled all of us. "He can't go there! You don't know what those places are like!" He breathed heavily for a minute. "Sorry. It's just that you guys don't know how Oceanarium treats orcas."

Mom patted my shoulder. "Arden and I have to answer this letter. We'll catch up with you later."

With that, they hurried up the path toward the office. I turned to Cooper. "OK, spill. Is Oceanarium really that awful? I've heard of it, but I've never actually been."

Cooper sank down on a rock. "Listen, Oceanarium has kept orcas in captivity for a long time. But that's not even the worst part. They force them to perform in shows. The whales have to do things that are totally unnatural for them, just to please the trainers. If they don't, they don't get fed. And they don't get to live in their natural family groups. They just live with random other orcas, so they fight and get hurt. It's *not* a good place."

Olivia and I exchanged a glance. That sounded awful. I didn't want to think of August ending up someplace like that. There was only one thing we could do.

Olivia took a deep breath. "I think we should see it for ourselves."

Chapter 7

"Are we sure this is a good idea?" I asked the next day. We stood in the bright sunshine, staring up at a wide blue-painted arch that read *Oceanarium*.

"I think it is," Olivia replied. She pulled me toward the entrance, making our way through crowds of families and vacationers outfitted in shorts and ball caps.

"It definitely is," Cooper said on my other side. "I want you guys to see this in person."

We made our way past tanks of turtles and fish, an outdoor habitat for seals and one for otters, and a large dolphin pool. Cooper led us up onto concrete bleachers that surrounded a huge pool on three sides. A large digital sign above the pool read: *Orca Show featuring Kaya and her trainer, Samantha!*

It was strange to realize we'd be seeing an orca soon. I felt more like I was at a public swimming pool. The water in the pool was so blue, and the concrete was hot under my shorts. The bleachers around us were filled with kids grasping melting ice-creams and couples aiming their phones at the pool.

Suddenly music filled the air, and a voice on a loudspeaker boomed, "Oceanarium patrons, welcome to the Orca Show! Please welcome Kaya and her trainer, Samantha!"

Gates I hadn't noticed before opened at one end of the pool, and with a giant splash, an orca swam into the pool with a trainer in a wet suit riding on her back. The trainer was almost surfing above the water, smiling and waving, as the orca swam rapidly around the perimeter of the pool. The crowd around us cheered as music played.

"The beautiful Kaya!" the announcer's voice boomed. The orca suddenly dove, flinging her tail up, and the trainer did a somersault and landed beautifully in the water.

As we watched, the trainer swam to the edge of the pool and jumped out. She tweeted a whistle, and Kaya swam over to a large white platform that extended out from the side of the pool, just below the surface of the water.

The trainer knelt beside the orca and gave some kind of hand signal. In response, the whale blew a plume of water out of her blowhole, soaking the first two rows of people, all of whom shrieked with delight. Another signal followed, and the orca flopped off the platform and back into the water.

My stomach felt sick as I watched the show. I looked over at Olivia and Cooper. They both had the same expression on their faces, like they were being forced to hold something sour in their mouths.

"Oh, oh, oh," Olivia was muttering. Her hands were clenched in her lap.

"I've seen enough," I told the other two.

My friends nodded, and we edged past people out to the aisle. Everyone else seemed enthralled, but I couldn't watch another minute. We made our way down the steps and away from the pool.

"Sick!" I exploded as soon as we were away. "That's sickening!"

"They're treating that orca like a trained dog," Olivia agreed. "No ocean water, no hunting, no pod, just a whistle and . . ."

She trailed off, pressing her hands over her mouth. I could see tears coursing down her cheeks.

"I told you," Cooper said. He gestured toward the dolphin pool we'd stopped by. "It's the same for these bottlenose dolphins. This is a totally unnatural place for an orca. Orcas are super smart. They have a whole culture within their pods. They have their own language. They're meant to stay together for their entire lives."

I sank down onto a bench and rested my arms on my knees. I stared at the concrete beneath my feet, where a group of ants were attacking a chewed-up wad of gum. "I didn't realize it was this bad."

"It gets even worse." Cooper was pacing now, as if he were too upset to stand still. Then he edged toward us and lowered his voice. "Orcas at Oceanarium attack each other and fight, which they never do in the wild. Some orcas have even killed others because they're just tossed in a tank together. They've even attacked their trainers and hurt them."

Olivia inhaled. "That's awful!"

"It's like prison. Imagine being thrust into a cell with a total stranger. That's what it's like," Cooper went on relentlessly. "Orcas never attack humans in the wild. It's a sign of how stressed they are in places like these."

I couldn't bear to think of August winding up at Oceanarium. They couldn't get him. They just couldn't. He was only a baby. He deserved to be with his pod, hunting seals and swimming hundreds of miles through cold ocean waters.

"We have to make sure my mom and yours are prepared to make the case to NOAA," I said, standing up from the bench. "We have to keep August out of here."

A man walking by gave us a strange look. He was wearing a wet suit, just like the trainer from the Orca Show, and his hair was wet. His face was familiar, but I couldn't quite place him.

Suddenly the man stopped, and at the same time, I realized who it was: Davis Hammond, the head trainer who'd been lobbying to get August. He was the one who'd sent the letter to SJS. I hadn't recognized him out of normal clothes and with his hair slicked back.

"Hey, kids," Davis said, offering us a big smile. "Checking out the show? It's nice to see you on Oceanarium's grounds. I hope you saw Kaya and Samantha back there. Pretty impressive, isn't it?"

I took a deep breath and glanced over at Olivia and Cooper. They both gave me looks that said, *Do it!*

"Actually we're pretty worried at even the possibility of August coming to live here." I hesitated. I'd never said anything like this to an adult before. "We think he'd have a happier life in the wild, with his pod. You have to admit, that's where he *should* be, right?"

The smile disappeared from Davis' face as if it had been sucked off. "As a matter of fact, I don't agree," he snapped. "You kids are beyond naïve to think that the orca could be reintroduced into his pod. And so is the rest of the SJS staff. You do know that it's never been done before, right? No orca has ever been successfully returned to the wild after being rehabilitated by humans. Your orca will starve to death in the ocean, alone. That's a long, slow death. Is that what you want for him? Is it?"

My face was flaming, and my throat was aching as I faced down his anger. I tried to swallow past the lump in my throat. Thankfully I felt Cooper and Olivia crowding behind me. They gave me the courage to say, "It's not what I want, but I don't think that's what will happen."

Without waiting for a response, I turned and walked blindly toward the exit, with Cooper and Olivia hurrying behind me. We had seen more than enough. Now we had work to do.

Chapter 8

I felt dizzy when I walked into the conference room at NOAA behind Arden. Cooper and Olivia trailed after me. We'd finally gotten Arden to agree to take us with her to the hearing by alternating begging and promising to stay silent. Finally she and Mom said we could go if we stayed out of the way and said exactly nothing. Mom had volunteered to stay back with August, but we were supposed to call her the minute it was over.

Two officials sat at the long table when we came in, along with Davis Hammond. Dislike rose in my throat as soon as I saw him. Beside me, Olivia narrowed her eyes and shot him a dirty look.

"Thank you for joining us," one of the NOAA officials said, standing. "I'm Dr. Chip Sheffield, the NOAA Pacific Northwest Executive Officer, and this is Dr. Lisa Grayhouse, our officer in charge of mammal stranding." Dr. Grayhouse nodded at us. "And I believe you know Davis Hammond from—"

"We know him," Arden said shortly.

Dr. Sheffield blinked, clearly taken aback. "All right then, let's get started," he said.

The grown-ups sat down around the table. Cooper grabbed a seat next to his mom while Olivia and I hustled to the chairs against the wall and kept our mouths shut, as promised.

"We've reviewed the facts of the case, but we'd like to hear from each of you concerning the best situation for the orca named August. Mr. Hammond, would you like to begin?" Dr. Sheffield said.

Davis leaned forward. "Thank you, Dr. Sheffield. I'd like to begin by pointing out that what SJS is proposing has literally never been done before. Orcas released into the wild after contact with humans never integrate back into a pod. They return to humans for food and companionship all their life."

Davis paused and looked over at us, sitting against the wall. I heard Cooper growl a little, low in his throat, like a dog.

"Oceanarium will ensure August lives a long, healthy life," he continued. "A *safe* life. He'll be protected from disease, starvation, and injuries from boats. He'll get all the best veterinary care, including ultrasounds and blood work. And he'll have plenty of stimulation."

With that, Davis leaned back and folded his hands on the table. I could tell he thought he'd made a pretty good argument.

Dr. Sheffield and Dr. Grayhouse were frowning and nodding. My heart clenched. Did they agree with him already? Arden hadn't even spoken yet.

"Mr. Hammond is right," Arden said.

What? Cooper, Olivia, and I stared at each other. Had Arden lost her mind?

"An orca has never been successfully introduced into *a* pod," she went on. "But we're suggesting something different. We want to reintroduce August to his *own* pod—to return him to his family. Mr. Hammond has made a good argument for August's bodily safety at Oceanarium. But he's leaving out crucial information. Orcas have a sophisticated culture and family system. They have their own dialect. They hunt, mate, and live together their whole lives. To keep August at Oceanarium would be like keeping him alive in a cell. Yes, he would be alive, but what kind of life would that be?" Arden spread her hands. "We're asking for a chance. We know it is a slim chance. But we want August to have a chance for a normal life, all the same."

I exhaled. On one side of me, Olivia crossed all her fingers. I looked down at her sandals. She had her toes crossed too.

Dr. Sheffield and Dr. Grayhouse scooted closer together and murmured to each other. I wondered if they could hear my heart pounding in my chest. I glanced at Cooper. His face was twisted in an anxious grimace.

The two officials' little conversation felt like it was taking a billion years. Finally Dr. Sheffield nodded, and they both leaned back.

"Thank you both," said Dr. Sheffield. "You both made convincing arguments, but we're satisfied that the evidence presented supports SJS attempting reintroduction. Dr. Harrington, please draw on NOAA for any continued resources you and SJS may need."

With that, Dr. Sheffield pushed back his chair and stood up. Davis made a face like he'd taken a drink of rotten milk. He stood up too and nodded at us, then quietly exited the room.

That was it. I couldn't believe it! I shot up from my chair like I'd been catapulted out of it and threw myself on Arden for a hug. Olivia and Cooper piled on from behind. I didn't care how dumb we looked. I was just glad.

Chapter 9

Once August's fate was secure, we threw
ourselves into feeding him and planning his
release. He was gaining weight and getting more
active every day. He zoomed around his pen now,
blowing and squeaking. His whole body looked
bigger, as if he'd grown in the three weeks he'd
been with us.

Arden came to find us one morning in the
kitchen, where Cooper, Olivia, and I were all

busy loading August's first morning feed into a bucket.

"Kids!" she called, opening the door suddenly.

"Whooa!" I juggled a fat silver salmon. The live fish were slippery. The salmon flopped out of my hands and slithered onto the floor, where it lay there, flopping.

"Sorry," Arden said.

"That's OK." I grabbed the fish and threw him into a bucket of water. He deserved at least a brief break before being eaten by a hungry orca.

"What's up, Mom?" Cooper asked, looking up from where he was scooping up more fish.

Arden had a big smile on her face. "I have exciting news for you."

"The release! August is being released!" Olivia burst out.

"You guessed it!" Arden grinned. "We met with the vet, plus Jason and Greg from NOAA, and they all agree with Dr. Roth and me that he's ready. He's gained enough weight. I'm sure it'll be sad without him, but you know we want him to go as soon as possible. The sooner he leaves humans, the better chance he has of adjusting to the wild."

"Any luck finding his pod?" I asked. I plopped another fish into the bucket.

Arden's face grew more serious. "That's the tricky part. We can find the pod through satellite tracking. A few of the other orcas had trackers on them. But then the pod needs to take him back in. His mother is dead, we know that almost certainly. It's my hope that the next closest female, his aunt, will accept him."

"If she doesn't?" I almost didn't want to ask. But I had to know.

Arden's face told us what would happen. But none of us seemed willing to say it aloud. Instead,

Arden took out a piece of paper from her pocket and unfolded it with a brisk snap. "OK, want to hear the game plan?"

"Yes!" Cooper said. We all stopped what we were doing and gathered around.

"We'll get August into the stretcher and lift him onto the crane boat, just like when we rescued him," Arden explained. "He'll ride on the boat, on that foam pad, but this time, he'll be partially submerged to keep him cool and moist. The cloths were OK for the short trip back to SJS, but they're not enough to keep his body cool and wet for a longer trip. It's eight hours by high-speed catamaran to the place we think we'll find his pod."

Arden looked up. "The length of the trip will be stressful for him. We'll check his vitals, but you kids need to know that even at this late stage, he might not make it."

My heart speeded up just hearing her words, but I nodded as if I were brave. The idea that August would die after all was terrifying, but saying that wouldn't help anyone.

"OK!" Arden consulted her paper again. "Once we've arrived at the pod's location, a barge with a crane will meet us. We'll use the catamaran as a base to help make a small, temporary pen, near the shore. August will spend the night in the pen, and hopefully, the pod will hear his vocalizations and come to investigate. Then we'll release him!"

"And cross our fingers," Olivia said.

"Well yes." Arden stuffed the paper back into her pocket. "There will be a good amount of that as well."

❦

After that, time seemed to move much faster. The next four days flew by, and before I knew it,

I was shivering in the chilly, pre-dawn dark next to Cooper and Olivia. Small boats idled in the calm waters of August's pen. The stretcher was ready.

This was it. Everything we'd worked for had come down to this moment. But I couldn't feel relief yet. August was still in danger.

I hugged my sweatshirt around my shoulders and pulled up the hood. The fabric was already damp with sea spray. A backpack at my feet held a toothbrush and a change of underwear. We'd spend the night on the catamaran once we reached the pod site.

"He looks good," Cooper said to us, trying to sound encouraging. "He looks strong."

I nodded. He was right. August did look strong. He was diving and breaching and chirping energetically in his pen. He'd been trying to get close to humans more frequently over the past week and I saw him now swim up to Mom's small boat, rubbing against it.

That was dangerous behavior. Mom and Arden were right. It was time for August to go. He needed other orcas, not humans or boats as some kind of substitute.

I felt a strong sense of déjà vu as I watched the scene in front of us from our place on the shore. Two small boats idled, Jason and Greg and Mom and Arden crouching in them. The crane boat sat just outside the pen.

It was just like the rescue mission we'd gone on to save August. The only difference now was the high-speed catamaran floating beside the crane boat. August would make the journey back to his pod on that boat.

"Let's go!" Arden swung her arm at the crane boat. I saw the crane operator give him the thumbs-up sign.

Mom and Jason took out a bucket of fish to get August's attention and tossed one into the water. The orca snapped it up and swam over for another.

"Please, August," Olivia said aloud. "Please be calm. Don't hurt yourself."

Mom and Arden and the other adults were calm in their boats, but I could see the quiet focus on their faces. They were being careful with every movement they made.

As he had before, Greg quietly unraveled the stretcher under August, and Jason drew it up and secured it on the other side. Mom signaled the crane operator. A whirring of machinery broke through the quiet of the early morning, and August rose—huge, dripping, like a giant baby—into the air.

"Oh!" I cried out suddenly. "I feel so sorry for him!"

"Why?" Olivia asked, putting a hand on my arm. "We're helping him. You know that."

"It's just that he trusts us," I tried to explain, watching August swing gently through the air. "He found this nice home in his pen, with fish and everything, and now he doesn't know what we're doing to him. We know he's going to a better home, but he doesn't. What if he's scared?"

Olivia put her arm around my shoulders and squeezed. To my surprise, Cooper did the same from the other side. We stood like that, linked, and watched as August was lowered gently to the basin waiting for him on the catamaran.

For a moment, no one breathed as the catamaran crew worked like lightning to release the stretcher and settle August into his water bath. We couldn't see what they were doing. The boat railing was in the way. But then, suddenly, the black, wet stretcher swung high and free above the boat and we all cheered. August was in the boat.

I grabbed the backpack at my feet. "Let's go!" I said to Olivia and Cooper. They shouldered their backpacks too. The two small boats motored back to shore, followed by the catamaran. Everyone piled out of the small boats and onto the catamaran. We climbed aboard too.

The motor revved, and then we were speeding out of the cove and into open water. Cooper, Olivia, and I hurried over to August. The catamaran was much faster and smoother than the crane boat we'd ridden on during the rescue. I could feel the cold, constant dampness of the spray blowing back into my face and hear the rhythmic slapping of the waves against the boat.

Arden was already at August's side, checking his pulse with her fingers and looking into his eyes. "So far, so good," she said, standing up.

"You three keep him company while I go let the captain know."

We huddled around August. He lay on the same thick, white foam pad we'd used during his rescue, but this time, salty seawater filled a black rubber basin all around him. It came all the way up to the top of his head where his blowhole was.

"August, you're going home," Olivia told him. He chirped in reply, as if he understood her.

We rubbed his head, his black skin squeaking under our hands. Cooper sang him a song about the whale and the octopus in the itty-bitty sea— one his mom used to sing when he was little, he explained. Then we all told August a story about how he'd find his pod and that his aunt might be his new mother.

The hours passed slowly, broken by the damp sandwiches we ate huddled on the deck and frequent checks on August. The sun inched up in the sky, sparkling on the waves, and then started back down again.

As late afternoon arrived, Mom checked August's vital signs again. She and Arden went into the cabin to look at the GPS, and then came out again. They were both smiling.

"This is it!" Mom said to us. "August's vital signs are steady. And we've located the pod. The captain's been tracking them for twenty miles. They're resting about a mile away, so this is where we stop."

We all squealed and hugged each other, and just as we did so, the engine quieted to a low rumble. We gradually slowed, then stopped.

I untangled myself from the embrace and looked around. We weren't far from the shore; I could see cliffs topped with dark pine trees in the distance. The gray waves looked chilly and deep, but this would be August's new home.

For a moment I was sad. But then I thought back to the aqua water and the loudspeaker at Oceanarium, and I was so, so glad.

Chapter 10

We had to get August off the boat and into open water as fast as possible.

"Every minute he's on this boat is putting stress on his system," Arden told us as the barge meeting us slid into sight. A crane sat on it, just like the one from the crane boat at the initial rescue.

Jason and Greg were hard at work stretching weighted nets and stakes to create a small, temporary pen right off the edge of the boat. That was where August would spend the night. We had to see if the pod would find him by hearing his vocalizations. And then we had to see what the pod would do.

"Done!" Jason said as he and Greg heaved themselves back into the boat. They were both wearing wet suits. The water up here was frigid all year long. Perfect for an orca, of course. "Let's move this boy out!"

They looped the stretcher, which was still under August, up. The barge pulled up alongside us, and we waved at the crew as they maneuvered the crane around and dropped down the metal cables. Jason and Greg hooked them to the stretcher as they'd done before.

Olivia and Cooper's faces were serious. "I want to feel relieved," Olivia said, "but there are still so many steps. Getting August all the way out here was just the first one."

Mom overheard. "You're right, Olivia," she said. "I'm glad you realize that. We still have a long way to go before we know if August will be accepted by his pod."

"Mom, could they attack him?" I'd been wanting to ask that for a while but hadn't been able to make the words come out. I'd been too scared to hear the answer.

Mom looked at us for a long, silent moment. She seemed to be trying to determine if we could handle the truth.

"It's more likely that they would ignore him," she finally said. "And if they don't accept him into the pod, he'll be right back where he started: alone."

The thought of August alone in the vast ocean was so upsetting. I had to push the idea out of my mind. This had to work. That was the only possibility I was willing to consider right now.

"All right, on three!" Greg called to the crane crew. "One! Two! Three!" He and Jason quickly jumped into the temporary pen.

The crane whirred, and August rose dripping from his bath, encased in the black stretcher. The crane pivoted, then clanked, and began lowering him down into his new, temporary home.

With a small splash, August entered the water. Jason and Greg quickly unhooked the stretcher. August swam out, and the now-empty stretcher was hoisted back into the air. Jason and Greg swam out of the pen as we all cheered.

August was in! He was another step closer to being reunited with his pod. We'd done all we could—the rest was up to the orcas.

❧

The night was long and cold. Cooper, Olivia, and I slept on the narrow bunks in the cabin, while Mom and the others bedded down on the deck. I turned over and over on the thin mattress. I couldn't stop thinking about August, swimming alone in the pen in the black sea, and wondering if his pod had found him yet. Above and below me, I could hear Cooper and Olivia shifting around, and I knew they were awake too.

Finally a faint light filtered through the tiny porthole in the cabin. We all rolled out of bed, cramped and rubbing our eyes.

"I wonder how—" I started to say to the others, but then I stopped. There was a noise outside—make that a lot of noises. Squeaking and chirping and whistling.

My eyes met Cooper's and Olivia's. Without a word, we bolted from the cabin.

Mom, Arden, Jason, and Greg were already on deck. They turned as we rushed up to them. Mom's face was bright and happy. She pointed to the water.

There, in the ocean, black fins were rolling and diving. The water churned with white foam and spray. All around us I heard the squeaking and calling of a pod of orcas.

"They found him," Arden said, her voice low. "They've been out there for two hours, calling to him. He's calling back."

She was right, I realized. I couldn't believe I hadn't heard it sooner. In the pen, August was swimming back and forth, whistling and chirping.

"Is it his pod?" I squeezed the railing to keep myself from shooting right up into the air with joy.

"Yes!" Jason said. A huge grin was pasted on his face. "It's them."

"Then, there's only one thing left to do, right?" Olivia said.

"Let him out," Cooper answered.

None of the adults contradicted us. Without another word, Greg leaned over the side of the catamaran. I held my breath as he jerked a cable. The temporary net collapsed, floating down into the water.

With one swift, beautiful movement, August swam over the top of the floating net. He was out. He was free.

"He's out! He's out!" Cooper yelled. In an instant, we were all cheering and clapping and hugging each other.

August swam quietly off to the side, several yards away from the churning pod.

"Why isn't he going up to them?" I asked.

"He's holding off. He's keeping his distance until they signal he's accepted. It's like good manners," Arden said. "He's being a very smart boy. And look! There they go!"

Suddenly the black fins were moving away in smooth, up and down movements through the water. I kept my eyes glued to August's little dorsal fin. He stayed in the same place. The pod was getting farther away.

Go! Go! I urged him in my head. *Go with your family!*

Then Olivia gasped. "He's going!" she exclaimed.

And he was. The little orca swam after the rest of the pod, slowly at first, then faster, closing the distance between them. We watched and watched until the fins grew smaller and disappeared into the vast, gray ocean.

Epilogue

The San Juan Marine Mammal Sanctuary seemed so very far away once Olivia and Mom and I were back home at Seaside Sanctuary. Looking out at the flat, white South Carolina beaches, I could hardly believe we'd even been there.

That land of rocks and pine trees and cold water seemed like a different world from the thick heat and palmetto fronds we were used to in Charleston.

Our time with August felt like a dream. It was back to real life now.

In December, I got an email from Cooper and suddenly, SJS and August rushed back to me as if I'd never left:

Hi Elsa—

I hope you're having fun back home. Mom and I want
you and Olivia to come out here again next summer. I hope
you can.

I have some big news too. Mom went out on the boat
yesterday and tracked August's pod. They found them. And
August is huge! You almost wouldn't recognize him. He's fat
and healthy and the best part is, he was with his aunt. She's
his foster mother, just like we wanted. We were right, and
Davis was wrong after all ;) We introduced the first orca
back to the wild after human interaction.

We did it, Elsa—all of us. Just thought you might want
to know.

Cooper

I closed my laptop slowly and sat for a
long time on my bed, staring at the wall. But
I wasn't seeing the striped wallpaper in front

of me. I was seeing August, swimming in the cold Pacific sea, next to his new mother—right where he belonged.

About the Author

Emma Carlson Berne is the author of many books for children and young adults. She loves writing about history, plants and animals, outdoor adventures, and sports. Emma lives in Cincinnati, Ohio, with her husband and three little boys. When she's not writing, Emma likes to ride horses, hike, and read books to her sons.

About the Illustrator

Erwin Madrid grew up in San Jose, California, and earned his BFA in Illustration from the Academy of Art College in San Francisco. During his final semester, Erwin was hired by PDI/DreamWorks Animation, where he contributed production art for *Shrek 2*. He later became a visual development artist for the Shrek franchise, the *Madagascar* sequel, and *Megamind*. He has designed cover art for children's books from Harper Collins, Random House, and Simon and Schuster. He currently lives in the Bay Area.

Glossary

condemned (kuhn-DEMD)—declared unsafe

enthusiasm (en-THOO-zee-az-uhm)—great excitement or interest

inhumane (IN-hyoo-mayn)—actions that are cruel or unkind

naïve (nah-EEV)—inexperienced and overly trusting

rehabilitate (ree-huh-bil-uh-TAYT)—when sick or hurt animals are treated and cared for; the animals are freed once they are able to live on their own.

transmit (trans-MIT)—to send something from one place to another

undernourishment (uhn-der-NUR-ish-mehnt)—when a person or animal doesn't have enough food to stay strong and healthy

urgency (UR-juhn-see)—needing quick or immediate attention

Talk About It

1. Elsa and the others need to be very careful when moving August from the ocean to the sanctuary. What are some of the steps they need to take to ensure August's safety?

2. While Oceanarium claims it takes care of animals, its goals are very different from those of Seaside Sanctuary and SJS. How are Davis Hammond's goals regarding the orcas different from Arden and Dr. Roth's goals?

3. Elsa is surprised at herself when she calls out Davis for his treatment of the orcas at Oceanarium. Why do you think she's able to talk to him the way she does?

Write About It

1. Cooper writes Elsa a letter at the end of this book, updating her on what's happened since she and Olivia left. Put yourself in Elsa's shoes and write a reply to Cooper.

2. Special care is taken to make sure August experiences as little human interaction as possible while at the sanctuary. Write a list of reasons why it was important to keep him away from humans.

3. August's rescue and release was very dangerous for him. Choose one of the characters who stayed with August during his journey and write a journal entry describing how he or she felt during the boat rides.

More About Orcas

Orcas are very social members of the dolphin family. Did you know orca pods can have up to 40 members? Here are ten more facts that might surprise you.

1. Orcas are found in every ocean on Earth. They are most commonly found in colder water but sometimes travel to warmer locations.

2. When first born, an orca can weigh up to 400 pounds and measure up to seven feet in length.

3. Orcas are the largest member of the dolphin family. A fully grown orca is usually 23–32 feet long and can weigh up to six tons!

4. Resident orcas prefer to hunt and eat fish and live in larger pods. Transient orcas hunt and eat marine mammals, such as seals, and travel in pods of 10 or less.

5. Orcas are some of the world's strongest predators. They eat fish, squid, seabirds, seals, and sometimes even whales!

6. Female orcas give birth to one calf every five years or so. They nurse their babies for one to two years. Mother orcas teach their babies how to hunt, and make sure they stay close until they're ready to swim on their own.

7. Orcas don't open their mouths to make sounds. Instead they squeeze air through sacs in their heads.

8. Orcas use echolocation, sounds and echoes, to communicate and locate objects.

9. Orcas can make unique noises. Each pod has specific noises that members recognize.

10. No two orcas are the same! Each orca has its own unique dorsal fin and a patch near its fin. Scientists are able to identify orcas based on their individual fins and patches.

Seaside SANCTUARY

When 12-year-old Elsa Roth's parents uproot their family and move them from Chicago, Illinois, to a seaside marine biology facility in Charleston, South Carolina, she expects to be lonely and bored. Little does she know that Seaside Sanctuary might just be the most interesting place she could have imagined. Whether she's exploring her new home, getting to know an amazing animal, or basking in the sun, Elsa realizes there's fun to be had—and mysteries to be solved—at Seaside Sanctuary.

Read all of Elsa's
seaside adventures!

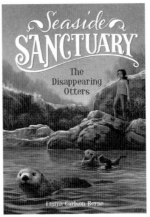

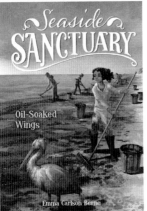

Use FactHound to find Internet sites related to this book.

Visit www.facthound.com
Just type in **9781496578624** and go.